Peebo
and His Pet Dinosaur

RÉJEHANNE de BEAUDRAP

AuthorHouse™
1663 Liberty Drive
Bloomington, IN 47403
www.authorhouse.com
Phone: 1 (800) 839-8640

Because of the dynamic nature of the Internet, any web addresses or links contained in this book may have changed
since publication and may no longer be valid. The views expressed in this work are solely those of the author and do
not necessarily reflect the views of the publisher, and the publisher hereby disclaims any responsibility for them.

Any people depicted in stock imagery provided by Getty Images are models,
and such images are being used for illustrative purposes only.
Certain stock imagery © Getty Images.

This book is printed on acid-free paper.

ISBN: 978-1-7283-6544-2 (sc)
ISBN: 978-1-7283-6545-9 (e)

Library of Congress Control Number: 2020911756

Print information available on the last page.

Published by AuthorHouse 07/09/2020

authorHOUSE®

PEEBO AND HIS PET DINOSAUR

Written by Réjehanne de Beaudrap

FOREWORD

Have you ever wondered what it would be like to live as a cave person and have a pet dinosaur? I think every child has spent time imagining this very idea during their childhood but author Réjehanne de Beaudrap goes one step further. Réjehanne has taken her ideas and turned them into several terrific stories. Her newest book, *Peebo and His Pet Dinosaur* is a wonderful and imaginative collection of tales about Peebo, a caveboy and his pet dinosaur, Rex. The stories are written especially for young children, but I know adults will love them too. Peebo and Rex have many adventures together, such as going to the lake and having special family times. The stories are written simply but with an eye for understanding how children think and what they do. The illustrations, created by a close family member, that accompany the stories are attractive and help convey what is happening. I know people will love reading *Peebo and His Pet Dinosaur* and I hope that Réjehanne will write more adventures of Peebo and Rex.

-- Mary Harelkin Bishop
Friend of Réjehanne
Author of *Tunnels of Time* and the Moose Jaw
Tunnels Adventure series

Interactive Questions for the Reader

It's beneficial to ask questions when reading stories to toddlers. This helps to increase their comprehension. Questions may be asked before, during and after you read together.

We have included some questions you may use during your shared reading experience. You will most likely have even better questions. These are just a guide to give you ideas.

Relax and just have fun together.

Before You Read

Before each story look at the title picture together and ask the following questions.

1. What do you see in this picture?
2. Who do you see in this picture?
3. What is happening?
4. What do you think might happen in the story?
5. Have you ever done something like that?

Here are a few suggestions while you are reading. Only ask the questions if the child is happy to answer the questions. Let's have fun while we read and learn.

Peebo's Pet Dinosaur:

1. Where does the story take place? Possible answers: In a land far away. In dinosaur time.
2. Who woke up Peebo? His Mom.
3. Who found the baby Dinosaur? Peebo's Dad and his friends.
4. What did they feed the baby dinosaur? Wild Turkey.
5. What would you feed a baby dinosaur?
6. Who was visiting Peebo's family? His Grandma.
7. What did Peebo teach Rex?

8. What would you teach your baby dinosaur if you had one?

9. What did Peebo and Rex do every day?

10. Where did Rex sleep?

Peebo's Summer Vacation

1. What time of the day is it?

2. What is special about today?

3. What is Peebo going to do after breakfast?

4. Where are they going for their vacation? Have you ever gone to the beach?

5. What did Peebo and Rex do at the beach? What do you do at the Beach?

6. What important rule did Peebo and Rex follow?

7. What did the family do before going to bed?

Peebo Goes To School

1. What was special about today?

2. Who will walk to school with Peebo?

3. Who will Peebo meet at school?

4. Why was Rex crying? Have you ever felt like that?

5. What did Peebo do when it was his turn to speak?

6. Who did Peebo share his desk with?

7. What did the students learn? What do you learn at school?

8. What did Peebo and his Mom do after school?

9. What did Peebo and Rex do for the rest of the afternoon?

Peebo's Thanksgiving

1. What did Peebo smell when he first woke up?
2. Who is coming to visit Peebo and his family?
3. What job did Peebo do to help his Mom get ready?
4. What did Rex want to do instead?
5. What are the names of the people who come to visit?
6. Who brought their pet?
7. What kind of animal is it?

Peebo's Christmas

1. What had to happen before the visitors arrived?
2. How was Peebo helpful?
3. Was Rex helpful?
4. What did they buy at the grocery store?
5. What did Rex and Peebo help Mom with? Have you ever done that?
6. Who was the first to arrive?
7. What did Peebo and Rex do before going to bed?
8. What are the names of the family members?

9. Who hid behind the Christmas tree?

10. What did Peebo say at the very end?

Peebo's Birthday Party

1. What was the special day on Saturday?
2. What did Peebo do to invite his friends?
3. What are the names of Peebo's friends?
4. Who were the first people to arrive?
5. What games did they play at the party?
6. What games do you like to play?
7. What did Dad dress up as?
8. What song did everyone sing for Peebo?
9. How old do you think Peebo is?
10. What important manner did Peebo remember when he said good bye to his friends?
11. Why are manners important?
12. How do you feel when people are polite and respectful to you?

CHAPTER 1
Peebo's Pet Dinosaur

Once upon a time, a long time ago, in a far away land, there was a caveboy named Peebo. One day, Peebo's Mom woke him up and said, "Wake up sleepy head. You need to feed your new baby dinosaur. Your Dad, and his friends, found him for you when they were hunting." Peebo slowly opened his eyes and was very excited to see his large pet baby dinosaur Rex!

"Hurry now Peebo! Dad is waiting for us so we can have breakfast together, but first you need to feed your green baby dinosaur. He is waiting in his pen for you. You get a bowl of water and I will see if we have some turkey bones to feed him."

Peebo and his Dad fed Rex some wild turkey for his breakfast. Rex loved eating wild turkey.

Peebo's Grandma was visiting. Peebo was excited to show her his pet dinosaur waiting in the pen. He was very proud to be the only cave boy to have a real live dinosaur.

Peebo spent a lot of time with Rex to teach him all sorts of tricks and good manners. Rex was a very happy dinosaur. He was so glad that he had his very own real cave boy to be his friend.

Rex was a fast learner and knew how to sit, how to stay, how to roll over and how to beg. He was really good at begging for food but he played dead the best.

Every day Peebo took Rex for a long walk so he would get some fresh air and exercise. Peebo and Rex were always very happy when they went for a walk. They were quickly becoming best friends.

Every night Rex would sleep at the side of Peebo's bed and they would dream about the fun that they had that day and all the adventures they would have the next day. Peebo and Rex definitely had become best friends!

CHAPTER 2

Peebo's Summer Vacation

Peebo woke up and jumped out of bed. "Hurry Rex! Get Up! Today is our first day of summer vacation!" Peebo was excited!

"Now Peebo, I know you are excited about going on vacation, but first we must have a good breakfast and you will need to help your Dad pack the wagon. We should be at the beach later today."

"Thanks for your help Peebo. We will be at the lake by this afternoon. I'm excited too!"

When they arrived at the lake Peebo and Rex went down to the beach to play in the sand and make sand castles. Rex pretended to be a big monster and stepped on the castle. They had so much fun in the sun.

Later, they had a BBQ of steaks and burgers prepared by Peebo's Dad. His Mom made some salad and had cold drinks for everyone. Peebo helped with the BBQ sauce. Rex's mouth was watering as he impatiently waited to be fed.

A half hour after the meal, Peebo and Rex went back to the beach and splashed in the water. They had fun but they did not go out too far. They listened to the rules.

Peebo's Dad was taking a nap after his big meal. Peebo and Rex got into some mischief and snuck up on him to splash him with buckets of cold water.

That night the family sat out to look at the night sky before going to bed. Peebo said, "This is the best vacation ever!"

CHAPTER 3

Peebo goes to School

"Peebo get up. We must hurry! It is your first day of school. After breakfast Rex and I will walk to school with you to show you the way. Hurry up now Sleepy Head."

"I hope you have a good first day at school. I already met your Teacher Miss Nettie. She seems very nice. You will also meet the Teacher's Aid. Her name is Miss Vickie. You will probably make a lot of new friends today. Isn't this exciting?"

When they got to school Peebo was so excited. He ran up the walkway then turned to say, "Bye Mom! Bye Rex!"

His mom said, "Have a nice day Peebo! I will pick you up later." "I love you." Rex was crying. Peebo had never left him before.

Miss Nettie needed to know all her new students' names so they each took turns introducing themselves. Peebo and the other children all sat on the carpet and put up their hand when it was their turn to speak. Peebo sat next to a cute girl named Maya.

Peebo and Maya shared a big desk together. Today they were going to learn the alphabet and how to count to ten. Later, they would have lunch and play in the playground together.

All day long Rex waited at home. Dinosaurs were not allowed at school and Rex missed Peebo dearly. Rex cried and did not want to eat. He just wanted to play with his pal Peebo.

When his first day of school was over, Peebo's Mom was there to meet him. As a special treat, they went to his favorite restaurant to celebrate his first day at school. They talked about his teachers and his new friends and everything that he learned that day. Peebo had a happy time with his mom but wanted to hurry home to see Rex.

When they got home Peebo ran up the walk calling for Rex. Rex came running, excitedly wagging his dinosaur tail and carrying his favorite ball. Peebo and Rex played in the yard for the rest of the afternoon. They had missed each other. Now Rex knew that everyday when Peebo left he would always come back to play with him.

CHAPTER 4

Peebo's Thanksgiving

28

Peebo woke up early with happy thoughts in his head. He could smell something good coming from the kitchen. "Get up Rex! Company is coming and we have to get ready!"

Peebo and Rex went into the kitchen. His Mom was just putting the duck in the oven. She said, "Be a good helper today Peebo! Your Aunts, Uncles and Grandma and Grandpa are coming soon. Please sweep the floor for me."

"No Rex. We can't play ball right now. We need to sweep the floor like Mom asked and then I am going to surprise her by setting the table. My Aunts and Uncles and Grandma and Grandpa are coming here today. Some of them are coming from far away."

The first guests to arrive were Grandma and Grandpa. Peebo and his Dad greeted them when they came in. Peebo ran up and gave his Grandma a big hug. "I hope you are hungry.", he said, "Mom is cooking an extra big duck!"

Next came his Dad's younger brother and his wife. Uncle Jamie was always joking around with Peebo and Aunt March brought her new Sabretooth Tiger Kitten named Fang. Fang wasn't too sure about that big green dinosaur.

The last guests to arrive were the ones that had travelled the furthest. Auntie Edna was Peebo's Mom's little sister. She arrived with Uncle Garb who was also a fun guy. Grandma was especially excited to see her youngest daughter as she was expecting a baby soon. Peebo would soon have a new little cousin.

Now that everyone had arrived, they sat down for their big Thanksgiving feast. They said grace, then Dad carved the duck. Everything smelled so good. Everyone was laughing and having a great visit. Even Rex and Fang were allowed to enjoy this great food.

After their Thanksgiving supper they had a really nice visit but it was soon time to say goodbye to everyone. It had been a happy family visit. They all waved goodbye and Peebo got another big hug from his Grandma. Rex even had a good time with his new friend, Fang. They all hoped to see each other soon. Maybe they would get together again at Christmas.

CHAPTER 5

Peebo's Christmas

Christmas day was coming soon. It was an exciting time in Peebo's house. A lot of family would be visiting but first they had to get the house ready and decorate the tree. Peebo's Mom and Dad did most of the work and Peebo helped too. Rex was very helpful in getting the star to the top of the Christmas tree.

Peebo and Dad went to the grocery store to pick up a big turkey and some supplies so Mom could do some Christmas baking. "No Rex! We don't need any pop and chips this time.", said Peebo. "We just need to choose healthy food for our Christmas feast."

There was so much to be done before all Peebo's relatives arrived on Christmas Eve. Peebo and Rex helped his Mom bake Christmas cookies and meat pies. "Peebo!", said his Mom. "Stop eating all the cookies! We need to save some for our company." Just then there was a knock at the door. Who could it be?

It was Auntie Edna and Uncle Garb! They came a day early and they brought their new baby boy, Rhio. Peebo was so excited and ran up to give them a big hug. He wanted to hold Rhio but Auntie Edna said, "Not yet. The little man is sleeping right now. If you wait, I will let you sit on the couch and hold him. He will like to meet his cousin Peebo too."

That night, before Peebo and Rex went to bed, they put out a glass of milk and some of Mom's Christmas cookies for Santa. Rex left some fresh carrots for the reindeer and they left a letter for Santa thanking him for whatever gifts he would leave for them. Then they went off to bed, but not before they had a least one cookie.

Rex and Peebo could not sleep! They thought they heard something so they snuck downstairs to the tree. Mom woke up and told them to go back to bed before they woke everyone up. She said, "It is way too early and Christmas presents can wait until morning." Peebo and Rex went back to bed but they were way too excited to sleep.

In the morning all the guests had arrived. There was Grandma and Grandpa who couldn't help but kiss under the mistletoe. Aunt March and Uncle Jamie came and brought along Fang. There was Uncle Garb and Auntie Edna who let Peebo hold his new baby cousin, Rhio, while he sat on the couch. Rex hid behind the Christmas tree. He didn't think anyone could see him there. Everyone enjoyed some eggnog and then they opened their gifts.

Finally, they all sat down for a delicious Christmas feast. There was so much laughter and fun while they ate and visited. Peebo even gave a toast. "Merry Christmas everyone and may we all be blessed!"

CHAPTER 6

Peebo's Birthday Party

Peebo and Rex were heading outside to play catch when his Mom called him into the kitchen. She said, "Peebo, do you know what day it is this Saturday? It's your Birthday! Would you like to do anything special?"

"Oh yes! Can we have a party?", said Peebo excitedly.

"Yes of course we can.", said Mom. "You go make some invitations to send to your friends."

Peebo and Rex went to his room and sat at his desk to write out invitations to his birthday party. He wrote one for each of his friends from school. First Edwin, then Vines and then Berna. Then he made the last one for his special friend Maya.

When all the invitations were finished Peebo and his Mom took Rex for a walk and mailed the invitations for the Birthday party. The mail box was very tall and Peebo had to stand on his tiptoes to reach the opening.

When Saturday came his friends started to arrive for the party. Vines and Edwin arrived first and then Berna came. There was a quiet knock so Rex opened the door. Finally, Maya had made it to the party. "Sorry I'm a little late.", she said. "You're not late! The party is just getting started!", Peebo said happily.

During the party everyone laughed and played silly games like "Pin the tail on the Dinosaur." Even Rex took a turn but he was peeking. Then they all went outside and played games of "Tag" and "Hide and Seek."

After a while they all came inside to watch a juggling and magic performance. Peebo's Dad was dressed as a clown with a big red nose and funny clown shoes. He made everyone laugh so hard their tummies hurt.

Mom called them to the table. They all sat down for some cake and ice cream. All Peebo's friends sang him "Happy Birthday." His Mom took pictures and his Dad made sure everyone got enough food. Rex wanted Peebo to hurry up and blow out the candles so he could have some cake. After the snacks Peebo opened up the gifts his friends gave him. He made sure that he thanked everyone for the gifts and for sharing his special day with him.

Everyone left to go home one by one. When Maya was leaving, she said, "Thank you for inviting me to your Birthday party Peebo. I had a great time." Peebo was very happy that his friend, Maya had come. "Thank you for coming Maya. I'll see you again at school on Monday.", said Peebo.

CHAPTER 7

Peebo's Friends and Family

CPSIA information can be obtained
at www.ICGtesting.com
Printed in the USA
BVHW090535090820
585866BV00002B/5